Once upon a time, or even twice, there were lands, and a sea, in which there lived seven dragons.

There was
the Blue Dragon

The Golden Dragon

And the Dragon of Many Colors

There was the Dragon Who Lived In the Clouds Over the Mountain,

and the Dragon Who Lived Under the Mountain.

There was the Dragon Who Thought He Was an Elephant

And the Dragon Who Wasn't There

In these lands also lived a young boy named Dax. He was captain of a fine sailing ship.

We do not know the name of the ship, but we know the name of the boy and that he was the ship's master, and so he was called *Captain* Dax.

It might seem strange that such a young boy would be ___ of such a ship, but this ___ so unusual in lands ___ there are dragons, one ___ ich isn't even there.

Time passes differently in such places, and it is impossible to say the true age of dragons or of the boy. He might have even been as old as you.

The lands, and the sea around them, were filled with wonders and with terrors. Not the least of these were the dragons, or the sailing ships themselves.

Captain Dax would sail all around the great Mountain Island, under which, of course, lived the Dragon Under the Mountain.

The dragon was well hidden, but you could always tell he was there by the great, black puffs of smoke that billowed out the chimney crater at the top of the mountain.

His brother Dragon in the Clouds would play with these, forming them into magnificent shapes that changed as quickly as the winds.

Sometimes the Blue Dragon, the smallest and most-friendly of the seven, would skip from the waves that hid him and join Captain Dax on his ship.

He brought fish for dinner, and would call to his sister the Golden Dragon, who would glint as she danced in the sunlight.

The Golden Dragon breathed down fire to roast the fish, always careful not to combust the ship's white sails in the process. She was not as careful with the clouds, and at sunrise or at sunset, when she was tired, her breath often caught the sky alight.

The burning orange, pink, and purple of the clouds never failed to bring out the Dragon of Many Colors, who thought perhaps that she was challenged in her resplendent beauty.

Once content that it was nothing more than Dax and the other dragons having their fun, the Dragon of Many Colors would snort a shower of sparks in disgust

The star-sparks would linger in the sky all night, helping the captain to navigate home. If the colorful dragon was in a better mood, she might blow Captain Dax a kiss, which would float, ethereal, lighting the whole of the night sky. Some mistook this for the moon, but those as old and wise as Dax knew better.

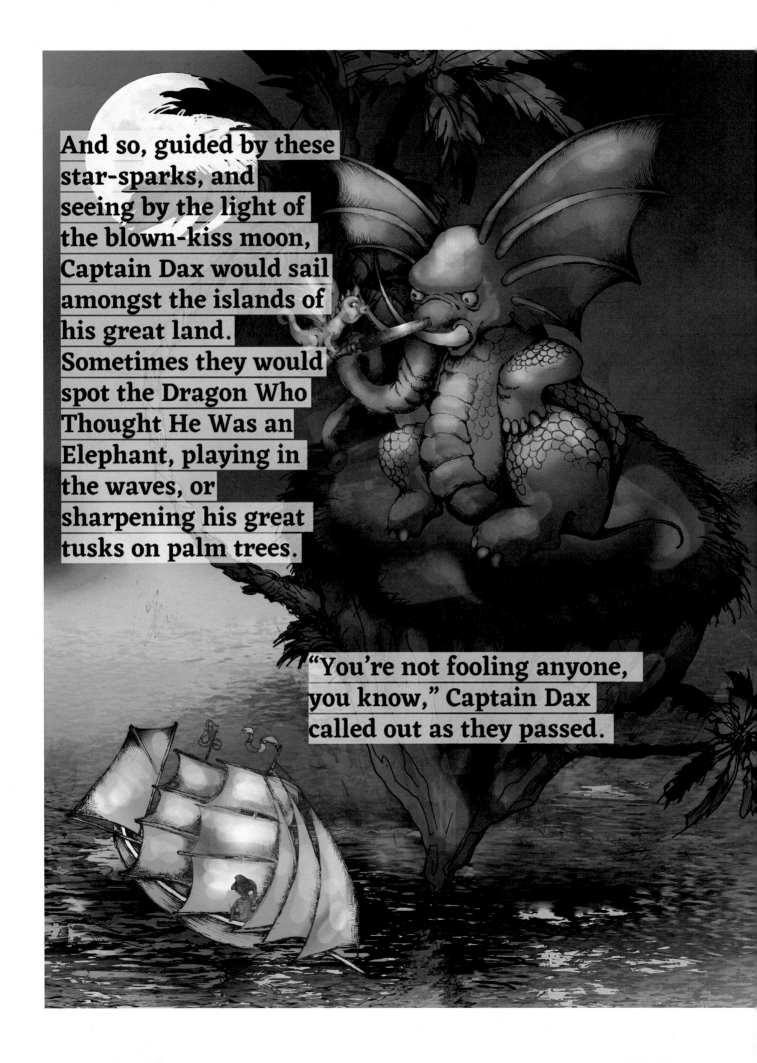

And so, guided by these star-sparks, and seeing by the light of the blown-kiss moon, Captain Dax would sail amongst the islands of his great land. Sometimes they would spot the Dragon Who Thought He Was an Elephant, playing in the waves, or sharpening his great tusks on palm trees.

"You're not fooling anyone, you know," Captain Dax called out as they passed.

Dragon
Who Wasn't There

"Do you think we will see the Dragon Who Isn't There?" asked Captain Dax during a particularly fruitful sail. He had spotted all six others in the same day and evening.

"I don't know," answered the Blue Dragon in his friendly manner. "We have seen many other signs and wonders on this trip. It is possible to see more, but rare."

"Our sibling is a shy one," explained the Golden Dragon, who was dancing overhead in a ray of sunshine.

"The Dragon Who Lives Under The Mountain claimed a sighting recently, but things are very dark where he lives. It may have been only a shadow."

"I thought I saw it floating in the sky myself," said Dax. "But the Dragon Who Lives in the Clouds Over the Mountain said it was just a puff of steam he had shaped into the form of a Dragon."

"So it wasn't there?" asked the Blue Dragon.

"No it wasn't..." Dax paused, thinking of what he had seen and not. "I only saw a dragon, who... wasn't... there..."

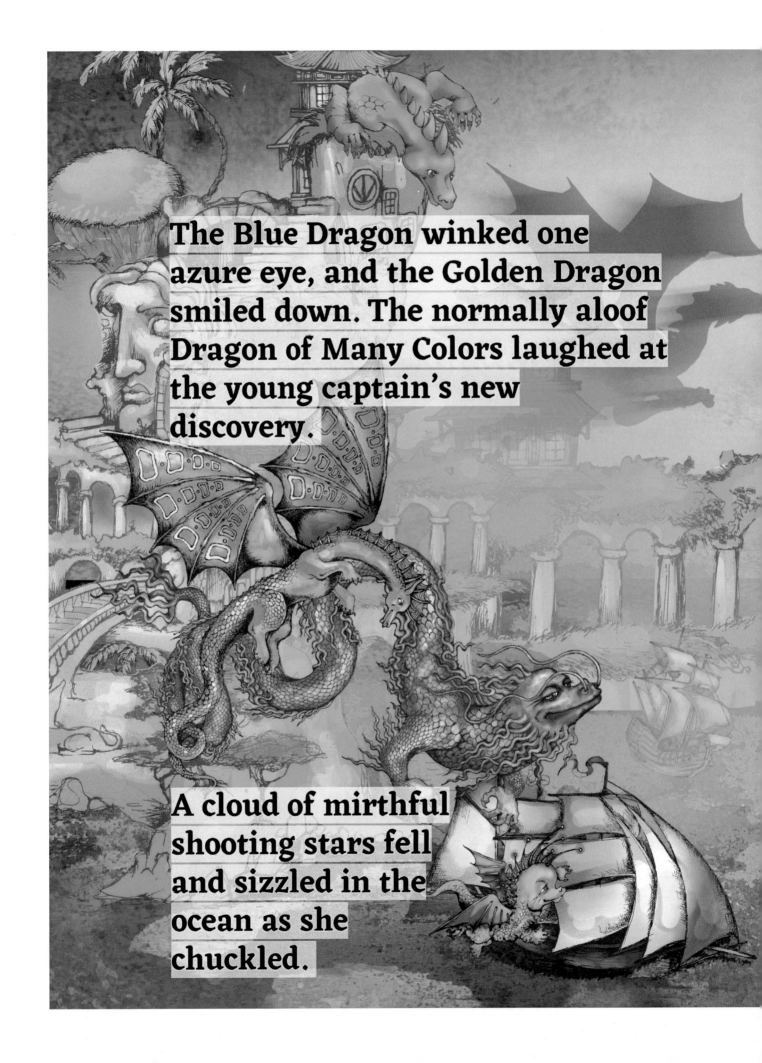

The Blue Dragon winked one azure eye, and the Golden Dragon smiled down. The normally aloof Dragon of Many Colors laughed at the young captain's new discovery.

A cloud of mirthful shooting stars fell and sizzled in the ocean as she chuckled.

The Dragon Who Lived Under the Mountain puffed away at this provocation, and the Dragon Who Lived in The Clouds Above the Mountain hid behind the puffs of smoke, quite pleased.

Even the Dragon who Thought He Was an Elephant trumpeted his approval, which was a dead give-a-way that he was one of the seven dragons.

Dax had spotted all in one day and night.

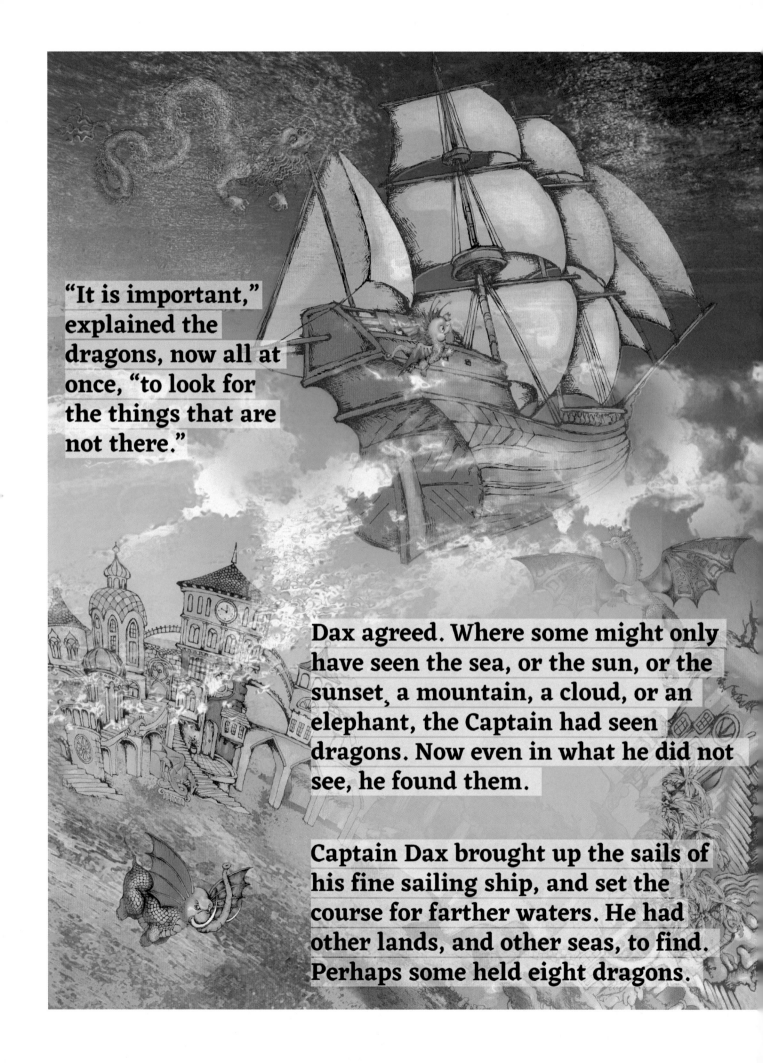

"It is important," explained the dragons, now all at once, "to look for the things that are not there."

Dax agreed. Where some might only have seen the sea, or the sun, or the sunset, a mountain, a cloud, or an elephant, the Captain had seen dragons. Now even in what he did not see, he found them.

Captain Dax brought up the sails of his fine sailing ship, and set the course for farther waters. He had other lands, and other seas, to find. Perhaps some held eight dragons.

Captain Dax's name is made from the magic combination of David and Maddux McLay, the children of the author. The Captain Dax Series and larger collection of Books for Brilliant Bairns illustrate ideas from philosophy, history, and science to the young hearted. Also there are dragons.

Books for Brilliant Bairns

Captain Dax and the Seven Dragons

Captain Dax and Dinner With the Stars and Moon

Captain Dax and the Biggest, Smelliest, Scariest Monster in the Cave

Captain Dax and the Ship of Theseus

Captain Dax and The Butterfly That Moved a Cannon Ball

Captain Dax and Rules of the Sea

Captain Dax and the Trolly Problem

The Rabbit Spirt and the Fox Spirt

A Child's First Book of Psychoanalysis

A Child's First Book of Brain Surgery

A Child's First Book of Wall Street Finance and Investment Banking

A Child's First Book of Feminist Literary Critism

A Child's First Book of Quantum Mechanics

A Child's First Book of Negotiating Peace in the Middle East

A Child's First Book of Aerospace Engineering and Rocket Science

A Child's First Book of Constitutional Law

A Child's First Book of Computer Programing and Silicon Valley Start Ups

A Child's First Book on Becoming a Navy Seal

Written by
Robert McLay

Illustrated by Helen Trupak

Look for Captain Dax and other educational children's videos on the Robert McLay YouTube channel

Thank you for reading, and learning.

Captain Dax
and
the Seven
Dragons

Made in United States
Orlando, FL
31 May 2022